She's Beautiful on the Inside and Out, But Totally Broken

By: LaTonya Gardner

Lightning Fast Book Publishing, LLC

P.O. Box 441328

Fort Washington, MD 20744

www.lfbookpublishing.com

The author of this book tells a fictional story of an adolescent who experiences childhood truma, to ultimately find her way as a self-aware and productive woman. The literary offering provided is fictional and derived from the imagination of the author. The intent is to give readers an entertaining read with life lessons interspersed throughout this literary work. In the event that you use or enact any of the material in this book, the author and publisher assume no responsibility for your actions.

This is a work of fiction. All characters and events are fictional.

The publisher, Lightning Fast Book Publishing, assumes no responsibility for any content presented in this book.

ISBN: 978-1-7348113-2-2

TABLE OF CONTENTS

LATONYA GARDNER

SHE'S BEAUTIFUL
on the inside & out
BUT TOTALLY
broken

Chapter 1
Different Love

The love I got was always different.

You know the kind of love that stings like the switch yanked off the tree well before it was ready to die, only to be twisted in the most unnatural of ways to strike across flesh, leaving invisible marks too deep to ever trace?

You know the kind of love that no matter what you do is never good enough, but always good enough to remind you that you aren't?

You know the kind of love that teaches you to hate yourself, to dread every breath you take, and to live life wondering... why me... or why not me?

Why can't the good love, the love that coats your soul, find me? Why can't I hear the laughter of love, the welcoming embrace of open arms instead of closed fists?

See, at Grandma Gabby's house, she'd give me a taste of that kind of love I craved, the kind my parents never knew how to give.

Her caramel skin, always wrapped in the nicest of clothes, was so smooth, it made you stop and stare.

But, if you looked closer...

You could tell from the soft calluses on her hands, and how her back seemed to bend under her weight, that she had worked hard... very hard all her life.

She'd gently touch my hand anytime she wanted my attention, and just her presence was enough to make me instantly feel safe.

See, over the years, I'd learn what it means to be kind from her.

Because no matter when I went to see her, she always greeted me with a smile, waved me over to give her a hug, and would hold me still long enough for her heart to almost whisper… "I'm sorry".

I loved her.

And she loved me.

Despite her daughter getting pregnant at 15 years old by a then 24-year-old man who should have known well better than to have sex with a child… Grandma Gabby loved me all the same.

When I was with her, my *real* Ma, I knew it was okay for me to exist. I knew it was okay for me to feel something other than fear. I knew it was okay, even when my cousins made fun of me. I didn't have to escape.

But at home, my parents showed me a much different kind of love… the kind of love that leaves marks instead of memories… bruises instead of blessings… scars and secrets and shame instead of security.

That's the kind of love I knew living on 908 Good Hope Drive, in the house with the split street separated by the fire lane. My birthday, August 9th or 8/09 as I called it, seemed like a sick play on numbers that cursed me from my very first breath.

My father's age of 24 and my mom's innocent age of 15 made my birth, when she was 16, equally a miracle and a crime all at the same time. But, maybe even in its fucked up dysfunction, this was really love…?

See, growing up in the housing projects, you see all kinds of love.

You see the addicts who love their drugs more than their kids, who would do anything to get their fix, even as their bodies wasted away.

Or the love the teenage girls fell for, with growing bellies, raising fatherless kids who, in turn, always searched for the love they couldn't grasp at home, on the streets.

Or the love that creeps into dimly-lit rooms at night, claiming your childish innocence with every unbuttoning of their pants and every swift movement lifting up your nightgown.

I knew all kinds of love…

See, even in the shadows of the darkness, I could feel his breath quicken. I felt the sweat on his brow fall through the thick silence in the air in my room. I felt the smoothness of the Strawberry Shortcake sheets on my back. I felt the heaviness of his body, as he climbed on top of me, his skin warm to the touch.

I remember looking up and seeing his face, overcome with excitement, as I glanced toward the shadowy, pounding steps running down the hall and through the door.

There I was with my uncle on me… and there my father stood, consumed with twisted rage.

I was 5.

He punched my uncle too many times to count, until the memory of him standing there, pants disheveled, body aroused in the moment, was replaced with images of his face bloodied, with red spots sprinkled all over the wall and wooden bedroom floor.

My father, exhausted from the fight, picked me up and held me so close that I could feel his heart racing with mine.

We drove in silence to the hospital, almost afraid for either one of us to acknowledge the tragedy of the situation.

I remember the bright lights, the long white hallways, the hustle of nurses going by on their shifts. I remember watching the automatic doors open and almost swallow me whole.

I sat patiently, hands folded on my lap, legs swinging back and forth on the exam table waiting for the doctors.

If I listened closely, I could hear the angry voices raised in the white-tiled hallway as they blamed my father for the vicious attack.

I'd never understand why they hated him.

It wasn't my father who hurt me... not in that way at least.

He'd hurt me in other ways that would leave lasting scars I could never cover.

See, my dad's form of love came by way of a beating for any little thing you dared do... or not do.

When everyone else mastered tying their shoes and I hadn't... he'd beaten the new skill into my brain.

Sometimes he'd beat me in front of everyone outside of our red brick house that had a green door.

In those moments, I'd stare at the house and try to escape, looking at the colors that always seemed to make me think of Christmas. Like the Christmases I had at Grandmother Gabby's house on the top of the hill at 1156 Good Hope Drive. She made sure we had a Christmas tree decorated with lights to drown out the everyday beatings. We opened a few gifts between us, to make up for the birthdays that passed with no parties. We'd share some warm, belly laughs and then like that we'd be whisked away back into our violent "normal".

I remember the warmth of Grannie Lizzy's house, watching the steam rolling from the corners of the pots scattered on the black burners in her kitchen. She was a great cook and she didn't believe in anyone going hungry. Her long pretty hair would sway, almost circling the aroma through the yellow kitchen. She always stood so proud, bowlegged and all, whipping up her delicious rice pudding in the biggest batches I'd ever seen.

I watched her stirring her pot of greens, looking over her shoulder to tell us it wasn't ready yet, waving for us to go back outside and play. We had the best home cooked meals everyday at her house -- and so would the whole neighborhood.

She filled you with that bone-sticking, soul-soothing kind of food that made your leg jump from the taste. When you were with her, your stomach always felt loved.

I wish she had taught me how to ride my bike, instead of my dad.

His love hurt. His love made me feel like nothing, no one... worthless... empty.

"This is so good," he'd say inches from my face, smacking his lips, mouth wide open, tongue stretched out, as he licked every drop of ice cream off of the spoon.

That was his favorite sense of torture. Forcing me to watch him eat ice cream, mocking me that I couldn't have any, while the words "You're not shit" seemed to wrap around my neck and squeeze until I wanted to die.

I remember being 8 years old, terrified to fall off my bike, but equally afraid to feel the sting of the switch. I'd often go flying over the handlebars after riding shaky down Good Hope Drive, to the bottom of the hill and around the circle. If I did it without falling, I was safe. But, if I tumbled to the pavement, entangled in the metal bars of the bike, I'd get hit -- and hit hard.

I'd go down that hill a dozen times, until I stood, all skinned-knees and bruised elbows, bracing myself for the spine-straightening snap of the switch.

"I guess you'll learn the hard way then," he said, standing over me, brown eyes glaring through my soul.

And I would.

I'd learn how to ride my bike and tie my shoes at the end of that switch. My heart would race anytime he raised his voice. And so I coped the best way my tiny body and broken mind knew how. I'd be kept company in the darkness of the night with wet sheets as the fear he ingrained in me took over and I couldn't escape.

Then, when I was 9, that night on the swings cut deep wounds that never heal and memories I'd never forget.

It was a warm dark night. The kind of night that you can hear the crickets chirp and if you look up, you'll see the sparkle of the stars with not a cloud in sight.

My uncle was getting married and we, the kids, were all outside playing.

I was on the swing.

And as the swing rocked back and forth, I could feel myself going higher. I felt free for once in my life. I could hear the hum of the streets in the distance, and the sounds of people talking in the distance seemed to put me in a hypnotic trance. The crisp air moved gently around me, through my hair, and around my arms as they gripped the cold metal links of the swing.

I was happy... maybe even too happy... because I didn't hear him calling me.

It wasn't until I saw his stout, bow-legged frame cross the shadow of the street light in front of the playground, that I knew I was in trouble.

With the switch tightened around his hand, he lifted it and came across my back, violently flinging me forward on the swing in pain. The more the swing moved, the more momentum he had and the more force he used to beat me. Suddenly, the chatter in the distance stopped and all that was heard was the sharp sound of wood hitting flesh.

As I went up in the air then slammed down into the harsh padding of the playground, I used my hands to shield the blows that rained down on me.

"Run... Run... Run..." my cousins Ivory, Keish, Hoop, Imani, and Cousin Leon screamed, watching my father's aggression threaten my life.

I managed to twist my body enough to get up and out of his reach.

I ran, arms flailing, knees buckling with exhaustion, seeming to only ever get a few steps ahead of him.

I imagined each step would get me closer to safety... get me closer to the good love... or, at least get me closer to where I knew I wouldn't be hit again.

But, it didn't.

I stumbled, out of breath, into the house full of faces I knew. They all turned, looked me up and down, then deemed that I wasn't worthy of their help and turned back to finish their conversations.

So, I learned in that moment, if I didn't love myself... no one would.

LATONYA GARDNER

SHE'S BEAUTIFUL
on the inside & out
BUT TOTALLY
broken

CHAPTER 2
GENUINE LOVE

"Come over here, so we can work on this," my third grade teacher, Mrs. O'Brown whispered to me, calling me to her desk to do our daily one-on-one session.

She was the first person, outside of my grandmothers, who ever showed me a genuine kind of love.

Mrs. O'Brown would take her time with me, making sure I felt good, making sure I understood my work, making sure that I was okay. I remember her sweet-smelling perfume that reminded me of open fields of flowers.

Her dark skin made me feel safe, even when I was struggling to read. Those days, in her class, I'd wish that time could stand still, just long enough for me to feel her love surround me and hold me still. It was something about her presence and her genuine interest in seeing me succeed that, in those early days, she was able to break through the emptiness my father had carved out in my soul.

I loved school then... in Mrs. O'Brown's class. But, when the bell rang and the kids scattered to their loving homes, I was reminded again that I was in a world where I just simply didn't belong.

My father made sure I'd never forget that.

I'd spend the afternoons at my Grannie's house, feeling trapped.

"She can't go outside after school," I heard him tell her. Why exactly he wanted to rob me of my childhood, I never understood.

So, as my cousins would run in and out, hitting the screen door, swaying in the afternoon air, I'd stare from the couch and imagine playing with them.

Sometimes I'd catch Grannie looking at me from the kitchen, almost apologizing with her eyes. I'd glance back at her, smile to reassure her that it was okay and go back to my daydream to try to escape it all.

But on the days my mom would come to get me, Grannie would break "his rule". She'd stand in the front doorway, holding the door open, motioning me with her open hand and as I'd slip past her, she'd place her hand on my back.

In those times, Grannie would give me permission to feel something other than fear, she'd give me the space to feel like I was loved, she'd give me the time to finally feel free.

See, when you're raised in a world where you are the inevitable target of abuse, you start to wonder if there is anything worth living for.

You start to jump at the slightest, unexpected move. You have flashbacks of his hand across your face because "you were writing too damn small." You fear everything that could hurt you and even things that won't. You start to simply withdraw from every feeling of being human.

And, that's what I did.

No matter how much warm love I'd get from a select few people during those times, it never replaced the loneliness I felt staring into the sea of faces at my 5th grade graduation and not seeing my parents there.

I watched the other kids skip across the cafeteria floor and melt into their parents' arms, with joy spreading across their cheeks.

But, me, I'd force a smile, shuffle across the floor and give my Grandma Gabby and Aunt Valorie a hug.

My mistakes are all that mattered to my parents, giving them a reason to hate me. My accomplishments... well... they didn't mean as much, and my parents showed me that.

But, things would change... the night my mother and father got into a fight.

I remember the crashing of things hitting the floor. I remember my mother screaming, veins popping out of her neck with anger. I remember my father's hatred spewed out of his mouth like daggers cutting through the night.

Then my mom left, slamming the door, and the house stood quiet.

My father had staked his claim and didn't let her take us. Maybe it was his way of continuing the punishment against me for being alive. Maybe it was because he loved us in a way so that her taking us away would have disturbed his soul. Or, maybe it was just his attempt to get revenge on her. I never knew.

He took his anger out on us even worse than usual after that. And, just as I started to give up and accept that this would be my fate, things changed again.

It was Fall, and as the school bus bumped along the potholes on the street, I watched the leaves float to the ground. The school bus stopped, a few kids rushed past me, nudging me accidentally with their bags. I stood up, turned slightly to look out of the window to see the house and I saw them.

It was my mother and Aunt Val standing at the bus stop. I had never been so excited to see my mother in my whole life.

She smiled big, opened her arms to hold me, and we walked away from his house.

That day, we moved into Grandma Gabby's house, leaving my father and his abuse far behind. And, he left us behind too, moving on to the Whore named "Bell of Good Hope." She slept with the men who she was involved with and their entire male lineage just to get a fix. My mother pitied and took care of her, making sure she was fed and safe from her abusive husband. To her now, taking $50 from my father, in the shadows of the night, for any and everything she could get, was done in the name of getting her fix. So, when we were forced to go somewhere because no one seemed to want us, she'd make sure to make my life miserable. All because she thought she was the shit with twin girls from my father and living free as a bird.

That was when I finally snapped and stood my ground against them all and fought back against the entire rest of the world.

And so it would be... I moved to Grandma Gabby's house and my siblings were the chosen ones, getting the privilege to live with my mom. But, me... she didn't want me.

At first I didn't care, because for once, I was in a house with people who loved me, with people who actually did things to make me feel welcomed.

We'd spend those days with my mom at my Grandma Gabby's house, a big carpeted house with an open floor plan that was filled with peace in every corner. Even with the cackle of the chickens running around in the backyard that was littered with used cars my grandfather sold as part of his side hustle, I felt at home.

That's where I secretly learned to drive, sneaking the cars away from the house, legs dangling trying to hit the pedals, smiling and turning the steering wheel with not a clue what I was doing. Or, other times, I'd take in the country land from the view of a lawnmower that I was convinced was my dream car, until I realized the crazy patterns left on the grass revealed my secret past time.

We would sit in the room and holler when Pop Pop, My grandpa Bally, a tall brown-skinned bald man from the deep country of Pohick, Maryland would say "scween" instead of screen and "scrimp" when we wanted "shrimp".

But, back then, my favorite day was Sundays, getting up, smelling the thick bacon sizzling in the black cast iron frying pan, with eggs scrambled to perfection, pancakes, and fried potatoes. Pop Pop would waddle out to the table, with his flannel pajama pants, pop-belly in tow, sitting at the table with his bright smile, elbows resting on the wooden table.

And, after breakfast, we'd go riding. We'd all pile in the black Thunderbird with leather seats, talking and feeling the bumps in the road, the air streaming through the windows taking us deep into the country of Howard County or through the backroads of Laytonsville. I remember the crunch of the Doritos and Funyuns they'd treat me to when we finally arrived at our destination, My Brother's Place, an old store they grew up going to. I'd sit on the concrete stoop in front of the store, legs dangling, chip crumbs flying, as my Grandma Gabby and Pop Pop sipped their favorite beers, passing the time telling me stories that always made my heart feel whole.

Those were some of the best days of my life.

I remember the black and white comforter, and the love in every stitch of the red, white, and blue knit throws that always made their circle bed feel like heaven.

But in the comfort of it all, I still wanted to feel wanted… by my mother.

Every day, I would get on the rickety school bus, watch the old country house fade in the distance and get lost in the stream of nothing but trees and grass. I wanted to run away from everything. I wanted to feel what it was like to truly be free. I wanted to be loved the right way, without the pain.

The emptiness I felt during the week always seemed to melt away when I stepped into my mom's blue Nissan Sentra on Friday evenings after work. I'd finally feel free from everything, especially when she dropped me off so I could hang out with my cousins. There was my first cousin Ivory who I loved being around, her showing skin my Grandma Gabby ("Ma") would never dare let me show the world.

That's when I started keeping secrets to protect people, so I thought. Maybe it was because I didn't value my voice. Either way, I held a lot of things inside, like the time my mom's new boyfriend cornered me on the basement steps, his heavy hands on my waist, lips planted on mine. I stood in silence, with Ma screaming down the steps, his finger motioning me to be quiet, and the fear of "that" night from long ago terrorizing my soul again.

Or there were the times Aunt Val tried to tower over me and threaten me with her presence, the times she would fight me because she needed to make me feel less than. I wasn't going for none of that shit with her, and I fought her ass back every time.

So, when I figured out how to get to DC on the Greyhound bus, using my saved up lunch money or the money I would take from people in school, I left the world that made me feel trapped and explored myself in new ways.

That's when I met Ronnie, a heavy-set, dark-skinned girl that coaxed me into seeing the world any way we could, even if it meant being reported missing by our parents. We didn't care. We wanted to live. We wanted to be free, no matter where it took us.

So, as "free" kids do, looking for good times and even better memories to drown out the misery and hurt we carry deep in our souls, we ended up in hotels or go-go clubs with Mike, my first love from around Maryland Ave NE DC, who spoiled us with clothes that helped to mask the years of our tortured emotional abuse.

But the reality was, nothing could replace the love I wanted from my mother.

She had cast me away like the blades of grass I'd fling from the soles of my shoes walking down the gravel driveway of my Grandma Gabby house.

What made me any different or any less worthy of having her love?

What made me deserve to be punished like this?

What made it so easy for her to give me up?

I was desperate to feel wanted by my mother, and if I couldn't get the love I needed to feel whole from her, then I'd take it out on the world and fight my way to get it, every time I could.

Before long, the backwards, backroads, stupid country kids I was always surrounded around at school when I was living with Ma became my punching bags. I made sure, when I lashed out to try to take control of my life, that I never showed any remorse or mercy, regardless of who was on the receiving end.

Once, I took my math textbook and felt the recoil of its pages as I hit the back of the brown-haired white girl's head, before she chased me and my cousin Melissa through the halls, threatening to kill us. We were hell on wheels together and they couldn't do nothing with us at that school.

Another time, I got high and raided my neighbor's refrigerator, even walking out of their house with a necklace, hitting the road without caring about anything.

See, when your fear gets replaced with anger, you do everything you can to take it out on the world.

And, that's exactly what I did, again and again.

I learned how to lie, how to steal, how to do whatever I wanted to escape the feelings I was struggling to understand inside.

The quiet girl who was afraid to do anything, the scared girl who would wet the bed at the sound of my father's footsteps, the crying child who was used to being hit had now transformed into a rebel who was determined to hide her pain.

"Get out of my class right now!" the teacher screamed at me from across the room, pointing to the door where security stood.

Because when fighting wasn't enough to disfigure my pain, I turned to more disruptive means. I became the class clown, cracking jokes, talking back to teachers... turning my inward hurt into outward expressions that left me constantly suspended from school.

Soon I'd escalate again... now seeking a sense of invisibility that fighting or getting kicked out of school could never match. And when I stole from stores, hiding the merchandise in my locker, I felt a surge of power I had never felt before.

That ended quickly when loud knocks on Grandma Gabby's door destroyed our weekend. We were chatting, laughing as we always did in the living room, not expecting who would be at the door. Naturally when the loud knock came, we all froze, confused, but still optimistic that maybe it was an eager neighbor asking for sugar.

Nope.

It was the police.

And they were looking for me.

I remember Grandma Gabby jumping from the sounds at the door, nervously walking over to turn the brass knob, and standing perplexed when they asked for me.

See, I thought I was too good to get caught. I covered my tracks so brilliantly. I was always careful. I knew that they could search my room at the house because they wouldn't find anything.

When they did had to leave the house empty-handed, I smiled inside at my new level of trickery.

Then the tall, white police officer barked at me, saying, "We need to search your locker."

I panicked.

They put me in the police car, bumping down the old country roads to the school. And there I stood, heart racing as they searched my first-floor locker, opening the gray metal doors, and watched everything I stole fall out and hit their shiny black shoes.

I got in BIG trouble that day and wasn't allowed to leave the house, but for someone broken like I was, searching for love in all the wrong ways, nothing, not even being grounded was ever going to stop me.

"Stop fighting. Do your work. Stop running away," is what Ma told me.

It was an ultimatum.

I wanted to live with my mom again and if these were the conditions, I'd live by them to be able to hear my mother's voice wake me in the morning. To be able to see her smile when I wanted. To be able to have her smells make better memories in my mind.

So, I straightened up almost as straight as the folds in my ROTC uniform I proudly wore after I joined the club. And, just like that, I showed the world a new (less rebellious) me and put my rollercoaster-of-a-ride freshman year behind me.

I stepped into 10th grade, in a new school, in a new home, and with the hope of my mother's love to make me whole.

LATONYA GARDNER

SHE'S BEAUTIFUL
on the inside & out
BUT TOTALLY
broken

CHAPTER 3

HAUNTED LOVE

3216 Whispering Court made me feel like I was home.

Sitting on the benches in front of the apartment building, doing hand clap games, making up rap songs with the neighborhood friends.

My days of running away had subsided, but the trust I had with my mom was still broken.

I wasn't allowed to go anywhere. And in the off chance that I could go out with my godsister, we'd steal from Kmart because a summer without a new two-piece everyday to show off my curves at the pool was NOT an option to me back then.

When I wasn't finding things to steal, I was in school, sitting at a desk, learning the ins and outs of cosmetology, pursuing my dream of being a hairstylist.

My godsister and I would go between spending our time cracking jokes about Ms. Johns' acrylic teeth in class or raiding the shelves of the Sally Beauty Store, stocking our hair/nail kits with whatever our sticky fingers could touch.

But, no matter where I went, even in places I had no business being in, I could always hear my mother's threat...

"If you get pregnant, I'll kill you," she said to me one day, standing over me, staring through my eyes and deep into my soul.

I knew then, loud and clear, that I couldn't tell my mother anything! Especially not when it happened and I got pregnant at 16 years old.

I hid that secret from everyone... except my god sister .

"If my mom asks where I am, cover for me," I explained, afraid.

So, there I was catching the bus alone, knees pressed together, feeling my childhood innocence slip away again, on my way to the doctor's office to get the $135 abortion.

I remember sitting anxious, waiting for them to call my name and to put this mistake behind me. The bright lights of the exam room comforted me, legs open, feeling my body drift to sleep when the fumes of the anesthesia took my away.

I woke up from that nightmare and drifted through the days.

Then the phone rang. It was my aunt telling me that I needed to go to the hospital. Something was wrong.

I remember as the doors of the hospital flung open, me and my cousin Ivory running down the hallways, peering into the rooms trying to find Granny.

And there we stood, me on the left and Ivory on the right. Granny looked up at us, trying to mouth something she needed us to hear. We looked at each other and back at her in the bed, helpless. We knew her time was coming.

"Everything is going to be alright. I'm going to do good," he, my father, whispered to her, his mother, placing his hand on her frail, shaking arms.

My father called me over and grabbed me with his arms wrapped around me, for the first time in love and not to hurt me.

"I love you," he said in my ear, and despite all of the years of abuse he had subjected me to, in that moment, I finally felt the love from him that I had begged God to feel.

But what happened the next morning, I'll never forget as long as I live.

The screams from my aunt's room down the hall instantly woke me up. Paralyzed in fear, I dropped to the floor, my soul crushed from the news I knew was coming.

Granny was gone.

In the midst of the saddened air that filled my lungs between gasping breaths and screams of pain, Ivory and I held each other crying for what seemed the whole day.

After that, I ran even more, stepping back to my 9th grade days, trying to escape the boring country life with Grandma Gabby. The streets became my makeshift home, believing the random (and dangerous) adventures I found myself sucked into would give me the love I was still searching for.

I got lost in the rings of smoke off of rolled joints or in the shuffle of the night going to the go-go's of the Ibex, the Taj Mahal. I'd sneak into places with fake IDs, hanging with crowds that made having fun their top priority.

Then "it" happened again… at 18 years old I was pregnant and so afraid.

While everyone else was excited figuring out what to wear to prom, I was ashamed.

I did everything I could to hide the truth. To hide the growing baby inside of me. To try to make that broken little girl inside of me feel safe again.

And, so on my prom night, with a mother that never took much interest in wanting me to feel beautiful, my Aunt Val helped me get dressed.

I remember how soft the criss-crossed back of my champagne dress felt on my skin, I remember how pretty I looked in the mirror in my make-up, I remember how it felt to suck in my stomach as tight as I could to hide my secret.

I carefully walked to the car, slide into the backseat and waved back at my mom and her boyfriend standing on the driveway.

We snuck away from prom to go party it up at the Taj Mahal and see Junkyard Band with my cousins. Even with the shame, I knew that I wanted to keep my baby... this time.

So, as my baby grew, I desperately tried to push my mom's threat out of my mind. Afterall, this was MY body, MY baby, MY life, or so I tried to convince myself.

But in the calm of the night, feeling my baby inside of me, my mother's words seemed to suffocate me and leave me paralyzed. I made the decision to let my baby go.

It was the morning of my high school graduation.

I put on a slim-fitting white dress.

I put on my graduation gown on top.

I took a deep breath and sucked my stomach in as deeply as I could and I left the house.

I'd hold my stomach, sucked in, barely breathing for hours, until the force of each squeezed breath left my body numb from discomfort.

And, there, in those still moments at graduation, me and my growing baby walked across the stage to accept my diploma.

Watching my father try to grab my diploma as my Grandma Gabby told him that it was mine to keep, no one knew the emotional struggle I was having deciding what would happen to my baby.

See, my first love, now locked up over a night of misunderstandings, begged me to keep our baby. He pleaded for me to have our child, leaving him a legacy he could return to, if he got out. So when I broke the news of my decision to him, I could feel his anguish race through the phone lines as the tears fell on his face, holding the phone receiver tightly pressed against his cheek.

When the day came to let my baby go for good, I got dressed, pulling a pair of light grey sweatpants over my growing waistline. I slipped on my shoes, rushed down the stairs, waving goodbye to my Grandma Gabby before she could ask me where I was going.

I remember rushing into the doctor's office, a little more aware of what to expect than the last time, but still terrified.

The doctor's office smelled like bleach. I sat nervously in the chair, feeling the wooden armrests pushing into my hips.

They called my name, I stood up, fixed my shirt, took a long, deep breath, and walked into the exam room.

I remember laying on my back with the bright white lights blinding me.

I remember closing my eyes, feeling a few tears stream down the sides of my face, collecting in my ear.

I remember the commotion of the nurses, the deep voice of the doctor, and the pressure I felt on my stomach.

And, I'll never forget, squinting through the flood of tears, over to the sturdy metal table and seeing the hands of my baby in a jar, all alone… discarded.

LATONYA GARDNER

SHE'S BEAUTIFUL
on the inside & out
BUT TOTALLY
broken

CHAPTER 4
SELF LOVE

For months, I had nightmares of my baby, now gone, and I wondered if I made the right decision.

To drown out the pain I felt then, on top of the years of hurt that had already made my soul its home, I tried to start loving myself.

I found love in tracing the edges of the credit card that gave me the power to buy whatever I wanted.

See, now I was an adult. I had no school that required me to show up and pretend like I cared what they thought. I had real freedom to do my own thing, all the time.

Then... the divorce happened and left me reeling, trying to make sense of a world without my Papa and my Ma together.

But, I guess that's what happens when your secret love child happens to take your wife's order at Popeyes and suddenly the buried lies surface in the most unexpected of ways and expose the truth of years of infidelities.

Either way... Grandma Gabby traded in the ranch-style country house on rolling fields of land with her husband for a five-bedroom house with my Aunt Val at 1300 Morningside Drive.

It wasn't the best, but it was ok for us then.

Eventually, when making $80 every two weeks watching my aunt's twins wasn't enough, and in between her pretending help me while staying an evil bitch, I went searching for something better.

See, my mom had bought me a car. It seemed to be her way of trying to erase the years of emotional neglect that had emotionally crippled me.

It was a white Nissan Sentra I called "Snowball" that seemed to unlock a new level of independence that I would do anything to protect.

And protect it, as well as the secret that led to me hiding cash around my grandmother's house, is exactly what I did.

It all started in the strangest way...

I remember walking into a dimly-lit living room, with a light on in the distance and the shadow of my cousin dashing from corner to corner in the kitchen. Mr. Milton J, his grandfather, sat rocking on the cloth sofa, blind for years and clearly oblivious to what was happening in his house.

My cousin stood, bending over the counter, looking at the water line in a mason jar. I watched him methodically mix the white contents on the counter in the jar, tapping the side of the spoon on the jar's lid. Then the spoon hit the counter and I couldn't take my curiosity any longer.

"What are you doing?" I asked my cousin as I walked past Mr.Milton J, stepping over his innocence into the kitchen and a world full of side drug deals and illegal cash.

My cousin motioned me over, scrunching his face as if to tell me to be quiet in case Mr.Milton J could hear us.

"Just watch," he said, sectioning off portions of the white powder, before putting it into small, clear, plastic baggies.

That was the first time I watched him make crack.

It was far from the last.

Over time, he taught me everything there was to know about making crack. I learned how to weigh it, how to sell it, even how to run it to his usuals when he was in Las Vegas with his girlfriend.

And when I got good, I'd make my own batches, sometimes using soaked macadamia nuts to get the crackheads their fake fix and to pad my pockets even more.

When the stash of rolled up dollar bills was too much for me to carry around in my designer purse, I'd sneak into my Aunt Val's boyfriend's (Uncle Sam) shed and tuck the bag far in the back corner, so the light coming through the window wouldn't be blocked.

Back then, I had money flowing from everywhere.

Cash helped to fill the emptiest parts of my heart, made me feel secure.

Cash made me realize that I could be good at something, even if it was illegal. I didn't care because it made me feel good about myself and that's all that mattered to me in those days.

It was October 9, 1997, and the squealing wheels of the red pickup truck coming down the hill as police ran in all directions threatened to take my livelihood and my freedom away.

"We got them now," someone shouted. In that instant, the world stood still, but moved at lightning speed, all at the same time.

I was paralyzed with fear, heart racing, breath gone, not knowing what to do to get out of the situation that was unfolding before me.

I remember watching the powder fly in the air, bodies grabbing whatever was in reach, bags thrown in every direction until the flushing of the toilet snapped me back to into this frantic reality.

I peered out the window, scared, watching my cousins hurdling over growing bushes, snaking behind the houses using the edges of the stream as their getaway paths.

That day was my major wake up call, and I listened.

From that point forward, I moved different and found other ways to get the money I wanted to give me the love I could never find anywhere else.

LATONYA GARDNER

SHE'S BEAUTIFUL
on the inside & out
BUT TOTALLY
broken

Chapter 5
Newfound Love

There was something about how he moved that drew me in. His name was KG. I never thought he was attractive, but I let him take me out to the movies on a date.

It was his swag, I called it, that let me know he wasn't a stranger to the game.

Before long, there we were, spending long nights cooking crack together, making runs, and getting more money than either of us knew what to do with.

And, when I found out I was pregnant, we both were actually happy. This time I would keep my baby and there was NO ONE that could scare me into believing I couldn't.

Times were good then, me with my bulging belly and all... until it all changed... again.

I remember the smells of the morning breakfast I was cooking, taking me back in my mind to those Sundays with Ma and Pop Pop in their country kitchen. I had cooked up the eggs, potatoes, slapped the bacon on the plates, and sat down to take in the calm of the morning.

"We'll be right back," KG said, waving for my sister and her best friend to come outside.

The lazy morning got the best of me and eventually I fell asleep, before the whipping sounds from the helicopters outside of my basement window woke me up in a panic.

The house was still. Too still.

Then, here was KG rushing in with a boat full of excuses like always, "She took the car. I don't know what happened."

It was my sister Isha, and she had gotten into an almost fatal car accident.

She was 16 years old and somehow had convinced KG that she could drive. But the swerve she made into the parked tractor trailer, ejecting her best friend out of the car, leaving her permanently scarred, inches away from losing her life, proved otherwise.

And a life would get lost that day, just not my sister's.

I remember seeing the blood rushing out of my sister's head as she lay in the hospital bed, pillows stained with the tragedy.

As I prayed for her to keep fighting to live, I could feel the cramps circle through my body, pushing me to grab the walls trying to brace myself for the pain.

And when I used the bathroom and saw blood swirl around when I flushed, I knew that the worst was yet to come.

That day I lost my baby. The baby I desperately wanted. The baby I had planned our entire future around.

But if losing my baby was the sacrifice that had to be made to save my sister's soul, then I know that my baby wasn't lost in vain.

It would be a few months and soon I'd be carrying KG's baby again.

This time, I was on bedrest for six months and not taking any chances. I wanted my baby and couldn't wait to run my fingers through his hair, with him looking back up at me with eyes full of love.

Other than the small belly I carried, my body could trick you into thinking I wasn't pregnant. It wasn't until the last three months that I saw my body swell with pregnancy as my baby grew.

It was a new beginning for me and I was determined to give my baby nothing but the best. So, ready for the new life that lay ahead for us, I moved into my first place. A place that was all for me, all on my own, in upper Montgomery Co. I'd stare at the mirror that lined the dining room wall, turning to the side to see my belly growing bigger by the day.

And on December 8, 1999 at 8:55am, after 19 hours of painful labor, I was wheeled into the operating room for an emergency C-section. The time seemed to pass so slowly until I heard it... my baby's cries. There he was, this beautiful, chocolate baby I called "Dunk" with a head full of curly hair, weighing 10 pounds 3 ounces, stretching out to a full 21.5 inches.

I finally had something I made... something that was mine... something no one could take away from me.

But the peace and joy of motherhood wasn't met with open hugs and helping hands. Instead, I was welcomed into being a new mom with my boyfriend's fists.

"You are not going to give me the money," he screamed inches from my face. I could see him ripping up the money orders I bought to pay my bills. With my two-month-old sitting barely 10 feet from us, as he straddled over me punching me repeatedly until my eyes were blackened, teeth shifted from the force of the blows.

"Please help me," I pleaded to a man in the parking lot, carrying my son, running with blood streaming from my face. The world changed when I looked at it then through tears, mixed with confusion, cloaked in deep pain, deeper than the bruises that covered my face.

He apologized, he cried, he bought me gifts and was careful not to beat me as bad the next few times.

One time he picked me up from work, roses scattered on the floor and Lifesaver gummies spread out into the shape of a heart.

He dropped on one knee, proposed to me with the tiniest diamond I had ever seen, shocked by what I said next.

"I'll say 'yes' when you get me a bigger ring," I said to him with defiance in my eyes.

He got up, shrugged off the rejection and returned home with a three-carat diamond that gave me no choice but to say "yes".

And so I did.

We got married on February 13, 2001. Nothing formal, or even worth mentioning. Just two people getting married at the courthouse.

"Will you come to the wedding?" I asked my father. It was a gesture to make me feel like I belonged for once and could enjoy the traditions that everyone else has to keep them company.

"No! I'm not coming. I don't agree with this," he said defiant and crushing me from the inside like all those many years before.

But, looking back, if I was ever going to listen to my father's advice, I should have that day and not married KG. But, I did.

And now, officially as his wife, he beat me regularly until all I had was blackened eyes and bruises to hold me close.

I wanted more for my son. I wanted more for me. I needed to find a way to escape. So, even with some fear telling me not to do it, I made a plan to fight back and reclaim the life that I deserved.

Over the course of weeks, I'd go from sleeping naked, to sleeping with shirts and pants on to hide the money that I was stealing from him to get my freedom.

I went from being his submissive wife, to being the strong woman who made drug deals on my own, who skimmed his highest paying customers to fill the shoebox in my son's room with the money that would rewrite our lives.

So, when I abruptly lost my apartment and had to move in the basement at my mother's house, I felt instantly defeated.

The Mall

The cold fell on the city and we ventured out to get little Kenny a winter coat and boots. I could hear Big Kenny's, little Kenny's father, in the distance talking on the phone to his mother.

They were talking about me. And now four months pregnant with my second child, I wasn't having it.

I slammed the car door.

I took my son by the hand, rubbing my belly, and we went into the house.

Without thinking twice, I hid my keys in the artificial plant in the middle of the glass table.

"Give me your keys," he said, standing with his hand in his pocket.

"I'm not giving you shit, ask your mother," I screamed at him, walking down the steps to my bedroom in the basement.

Kenny sat on the last few steps, cornrows dangling brushing the collar of his Polo shirt. I remember looking up to see his father push past him, storming down the stairs before pushing me off the last step.

I caught myself just enough to brace me from hitting my pregnant stomach on the floor. Now, on my knees, he stood over me, and I could feel his gaze bear down on me, his hands clenched in rage.

Before he had a chance to bruise my soul again, a deep sense of courage came over me and I hit him hard enough to make him stumble.

He gained his balance, put his hand in his waistband… and then I saw it… the gun.

I still remember the coldness of the metal of the gun pushed against my temple. I knew then that it wouldn't be fists flying, destroying my self worth, but it would be bullets to tear through my flesh and end my life, right there in front of my child.

"If you got the balls, then do it," I threatened him, glancing over to see my baby full of the horror of the moment, gripping the carpeted steps.

See, KG had witnessed his father stabbed to death, the result of an affair turned to murder.

And for him to thrust his own blood into the same tragic cycle filled me with calming anger that made me not fear what would happen next.

As soon as he moved the gun enough for me to turn my head, I snapped. I wanted him and the whole world to know that I would not take another beating ever from anyone.

I fought back for the little girl left broken and unloved from my childhood.

I fought back for the babies I gave up for fear of my mother hating me.

I fought back for the years of thinking that I had to be his punching bag in order for him to love me.

I fought back to protect my son's stolen innocence from having to see his mother abused.

I fought back until I was too exhausted to keep fighting.

"Please stop, you're going to lose your baby," is all I could hear before I blacked out, repeatedly smashing KG's head into the steps leading up to the living room.

But the drama of the relationship wouldn't end then. Or, even after the mysterious gunshot that claimed a man's life outside of my son's fourth birthday party.

With the pressure of an impending court case and the fear of what may lie ahead for me, my son, and my unborn child, I entered the Betty Anne Krahnke Center for Women and never looked back.

"What the fuck are you doing smoking them cigarettes?" I'd yell at her, watching the smoke circles whip around her head. Her name was Tanya and her and I had an unspeakable bond that made my 60 days in the shelter somewhat more bearable.

I'd spend the last few weeks of my pregnancy imagining what life, without abuse, would be like for me and my two sons.

I wasn't sure what the future held, but I knew it had to be better than my past.

My Delivery

I wanted to take back control, and that included when I had my son. I didn't want my husband to be there. I didn't trust him. I didn't need him. I wanted to start over by myself.

I was induced the morning of July 21, 2003. And with my husband's face pushed up against the glass, watching my baby be delivered, without him there to hold him, I fought back.

My wounds healed from my delivery and I grew stronger every minute. It was in the comfort of the off-white couch with the big pillows that I got the courage to enact my plan to leave my husband reeling with the same emptiness he drenched my young adult life with.

"What makes you think this baby is yours?" I said, face twisted with vengeance and bitterness.

"Stop playing," he laughed with confusion.

"You ever heard… Mommy's baby, daddy's maybe?" the words rolled off my tongue with a sharpness that destroyed his false sense of pride.

"What are you talking about?" he still laughing, half angry and hurt.

"Whatever, I need money for the new place," I demanded to break the awkwardness in the room.

"How much?" he asked now somehow convinced that we would be a family again.

"$3,000," I said confidently, staring him straight into his eyes, cradling my baby to my chest.

He'd give me the money I needed for my new place, but what he didn't know was he was not part of my new journey.

LATONYA GARDNER

SHE'S BEAUTIFUL
on the inside & out
BUT TOTALLY
broken

CHAPTER 6
FAKE LOVE

I'd spend a year in the Rental Assistance Program, finding my way through life, now with two growing boys.

I made ends meet how I had to… being a young, attractive woman… you know how it goes...

I figured out the game and I played it well.

And if I saw fast money coming, I'd make you feel like a million dollars.

Whether I had to use my words, my body, or my personality to make you feel on top of the world, I would turn on an Oscar award-winning performance every time.

That's what I did to keep money flowing into my household.

I kept them in rotation to make sure I had what I needed. Some of them I did like… others were disposable.

With one, there was something about how the light from the club cascaded off his head as he pushed up on his girlfriend, that turned me on. His height and his big hands made me feel secure and so did the money that he gave me to make sure I was always good. He was an older guy and he knew just how to take care of me and keep me pacified as not just his lover, but also his friend.

The "other" guy, a burly, homely-looking truck driver, would spoil me too when he could, giving me money for the caring words

I'd feed him to make him feel wanted. I never thought he was attractive, but the pain that I could feel he carried drew me in, so I went along with the charade of it all just to provide for my sons.

I'd got good at playing the game, telling people what they wanted to hear, making them view me as they wanted to view me, giving me what they knew I needed, until my divorce was finalized on June 3, 2006.

And, then between working at the Acura Dealership in Montgomery Co, fighting through traffic from Landover, I focused in on raising my boys.

I wanted to give them the world.

I wanted to keep them safe.

I wanted to guarantee that they would always know I loved them, even when times were hard and I struggled with the brokenness I felt inside.

No matter how hard things got, I always knew that giving up my boys was never an option.

And, so I went to work and did the best I could to give them the life I never had, a life full of things I yearned for as the quiet little girl who would wet the bed for fear that my father's anger would hurt too bad.

LATONYA GARDNER

SHE'S BEAUTIFUL
on the inside & out
BUT TOTALLY
broken

CHAPTER 7
UNCONDITIONAL LOVE

The rumors started to spread amongst employees on the job I was working, faster than anyone could contain. We'd be out of a job soon, I remember telling myself, snapping me back into the reality that I was a single mom of two boys, 8 and 12 years old.

I wanted the best for my boys and to give them the life and the love I never had.

So, I knew I had to do anything I could to provide for my sons.

And, that's exactly what I did.

I started my own business, Helping Loving Hands, LLC on September 14, 2011. It was the blending of all of my passions into one and the birth of all of my dreams come true. This was a residential cleaning business in conjunction with providing care takers for the elderly.

I'd spend my days cleaning houses and caring for my elderly patient, aptly-named "Brother". And, let me tell you… Brother was a card and a character wrapped up into one.

As a 91-year-old man, a World War I and World War II veteran, he didn't take shit from nobody. Plus, even on his bad days he was more mobile than anyone thought and would love to eat my cooking. His favorite was always my fried fish. I'd batter it up and sit back to watch him eat every piece on his plate, licking his fingers in delight.

Every day when he wasn't ready to take a shower he would cuss me out, spit flying from the corners of his mouth turned up in anger. I was always extra careful with him and can still hear him shuffling along in the aisles of Walmart on our weekly trips to get his hygiene products and his hard candy peppermints.

I made sure to make his last days comfortable and when he passed away in January 10, 2015, my business started to dwindle down until I had to stop it for good.

New Beginnings

No matter what was going on in my life, I made sure my boys were taken care of, by any means necessary.

And before long I saw my boys thriving like never before.

Ms. Apple, Kenny's teacher, tested him and was surprised to see that his scores were off the charts. I always knew Kenny was gifted. Through the years, I had invested in his growth and development in every way I could.

With their father in jail, I worked hard to give my boys the stable foundation they needed to grow and shine.

Coach Walt and Coach Bo were the father figures both of my sons never had, and I was grateful for their support in encouraging them and nurturing them to become star athletes.

On the field is where they shined. They shined past the days of me working 12 hours to provide. They shined past their father's absence in their lives. They shined past all the emptiness I felt growing up as a child. They shined past all the years of physical abuse that broke my young soul.

Every chance I could get, I watched my babies shine from end zone to end zone as strong free safety and corner football players.

Even as a freshman at Blake High School Kenny was getting scouted for Division 3 schools, and those offers quickly merged into Division 2 and even Division 1 school offers.

But even from the stands, jumping and screaming in excitement when my sons touched the ball on the field, I could feel the shreds of disappointment in me, the years of longing for love, and the memories of my lost babies that I loved.

For years, without the drama of dealing with closed fists and the insecurity of my abusive marriage, I finally felt at ease.

Until one day… the phone rang.

It was K-Dog.

He was out of federal prison and had accepted my mom's unexpected invitation to Thanksgiving dinner. He had one plan in mind… he wanted to rekindle a flame that had been extinguished years before.

One time in his life, K-Dog saw his son on the field, in an element where he could achieve what his father never could show him or ever reach.

It was the school's homecoming game and the murmur of the crowd fell into a silent hush, then erupted into a loud roar as Kenny carried the ball some 70 yards to a touchdown, me screaming and running with him down the sidelines.

As Kenny walked off the field, wiping the sweat from his brow, he hopped over the set of stairs, took a deep breath, looked through his father and kept walking – looking for me to give him our celebratory hug.

In that moment, my soul smiled, and I knew that I had done something right and that my boys knew my unconditional love for them.

SHE'S BEAUTIFUL
on the inside & out
BUT TOTALLY
broken

Chapter 8
Forever Love

I always loved chocolate babies. I remember when Kenny was first born, holding him and looking at his black curls fall over his soft forehead.

I loved my kids more than life itself, and rumors spread that my son's girlfriend was expecting.

He was a star athlete. He was going away to college to play football on a full scholarship at Old Dominion University. And now, he was going to be a father.

"Is your daughter pregnant by my son?" I asked his girlfriend's mother, partly hoping she would be, but equally worried about what it would mean for my son's future.

"No, my daughter is not", she said with a confident smirk, convincing me to not believe what everyone was telling me. Also with her bitterness of the fact my brother no longer wanted to deal with her. Some lines shouldn't ever be crossed from the up. My son's girlfiend's mother should have never dealt with my brother. The scent of money on my son pushed her to get solid footing in his future.

Weeks would pass, my son would move into school and I was excited to see him thrive in a new place, with new opportunities, with a whole new world at his fingertips.

Then the truth came out.

She was pregnant, with a girl, due in October 2018.

But, then the drama began.

It started with lies about my son, spiraling into allegations of domestic violence and threats. And, in the midst of everything, with the world seeming to fall apart in drama, my granddaughter, Sugar Ma was born.

With all the lies told around her birth, I needed to ease my mind and put the truth to rest.

So when a DNA test confirmed she was our own flesh and blood, I instantly fell in love with the world again through her chocolate cheeks and all of her 7 pounds, 2 ounces that came bursting into the world at 11ish on October 3, 2018.

And since the day she graced this Earth, I've promised to love her unconditionally and give her the world just like I gave it to my sons.

She is my Sugar Ma and I am her Honey.

Even despite the drama, and the custody battles to make sure my son could be the best father to his daughter, I've learned to forgive, but never forget.

The further my son's girlfriend's mother stayed from them, the better life seemed to get for them. And I was happy.

So as they packed up everything and moved my Sugar Ma to Miami, I waved them off seeing my first born holding his own baby in his arms, going off into the new world he created for his own little family and still going to school.

LATONYA GARDNER

SHE'S BEAUTIFUL
on the inside & out
BUT TOTALLY
broken

CHAPTER 9

BROKEN LOVE

I've always seemed to draw people to me, like a magnet to metal. Some stayed and saw me through life, but others floated in and out like falling feathers in the wind.

One minute, I had friends that I called sisters. And, the next minute, their vicious words and hate for me would surface in the most unusual of ways.

Jealousy always seemed to be something that followed me in my life. Like the time my ex-husband decided to get married on my birthday, or the name that he chose for his child with another woman to spite me.

I was the shit and have always been the shit. It's not my fault the world couldn't handle it.

Like all the fights and arguing I had to endure with my Aunt Val. In the same way, other people came to me, and they also left me broken, left me questioning what was wrong with me, left me wondering why I couldn't feel the real love I know I deserved.

So, I'd go in and out of relationships, some faster than others, but with a feeling that somehow I didn't belong where I was.

That's the thing with growing up with a father that would torment you for his pleasure and a mother that never was emotionally there... you have this way of just feeling chronic emptiness.

When Kenny was born, my chocolate baby with beautiful hair, I dreaded going to see Aunt Grace and her dysfunctional family. If your baby was ugly, she would tell you, so you never had to worry about questioning it.

Despite knowing that I would lash out if she even looked sideways at my pride and joy, I still went and took him with me.

During the first 7 months of his life, I trusted no one with him, I'd barely leave him out of my sight long enough to go to the restroom. So, the thought of presenting him for Aunt Grace to say something about his appearance had me on edge.

I remember walking across the big grassy lawn to where she was sitting as she waved me and my cousin over, saying, "Let me see that baby."

It was almost as if time had stood still as she looked him up and down with her green eyes and then finally said, "That's a beautiful baby. Look at this handsome baby!"

And if Aunt Grace said it, then it was truth. But as she smiled and stared in awe at him, as it always happened, somebody had something else to say.

See I never was allowed to be the center of attention in a positive way, I had to be the scapegoat, the whipping boy, the one that people HAD to talk about.

That's what happens when all you get is broken, shattered, twisted love.

All this has made me stronger, made me trust people a lot less, but it has also been a constant reminder that I am more powerful than what I even believe and one day I'll step into the real unconditional love that I know I deserve.

LATONYA GARDNER

SHE'S BEAUTIFUL
on the inside & out
BUT TOTALLY
broken

Chapter 10
My Truth

I've felt many types of love through my life. Some of them I'd long to feel again, like the genuine love from my Pop Pop & Granny (Lizzy). Other types of love I'd rather forget.

Taken together, they have shaped who I am, where I've gone in life, how I love, and how I view the world.

The words on these pages, contained in this book, are my words. They are my truths. They are my way of healing from the past so that I can run with open arms into my future.

I wrote this book for no one other than myself, and the freedom I feel in this moment having you read what I've often buried deep in craters of pain that I've carried with me is a feeling I can't describe.

Because, despite the fleeting and tainted love I've felt my whole life, this book, my words, and my memories are mine to keep. They can never be taken away from me.

If you've made it this far in my literary journey, then you've experienced my darkest moments and you've read through the joy and accomplishments of my life too.

At the end, what we have in our hearts and in our minds is all that we will take with us.

And this is the power of this book and the power of me being able to release MY TRUTH.

Once a fool get wise a hustler can't stand a chance.

Lizzy Burton (Granny)

LATONYA GARDNER

SHE'S BEAUTIFUL
on the inside & out
BUT TOTALLY
broken

ABOUT THE AUTHOR

LaTonya Gardner is a breakout author, a strong single mother of two thriving sons, and the proud grandmother to the brightest baby in the world. As a straight hustler, she went from suffering physical abuse at the hands of her father, to seeking love in all the wrong places, to finding her way on her own and starting multiple profitable businesses. She is the example of perseverance, determination, and the power of unconditional self-love in sparking real healing and breaking generational curses.